PO MALU

...Silent Night...

A Novel
New Edition, 2019

Semisi Pone

Note: PO MALU was first published in New Zealand in 2013 and is available under two original titles PO MALU and SILENT NIGHT from amazon.com in ebook and print formats. The writer had written the original versions in the Polynesian storytelling style of FANANGA which tell a story without too many superfluous details. This new edition is written in the style of English and American novels, with more detail of emotion, surroundings, dress and odd behavior to give the story more 'color'. Other originals are available as a free reading book for kids, in blurb.com, as part of the writer's Project Revival Charity Trust (Inc) reading programme, and as a pdf ebook from www.wheelers.co.nz.

CONTENT

Chapter One....

A GRANDFATHER'S LEGACY

The 50 year Tongan Civil War, began with the assassination of Tuku'aho, the 14th Tu'i Kanokupolu in 1799. Tuku'aho, although a great warrior and leader, was a very cruel man; many of the rumors written about him suggest he punish some of his subordinates by tying some of them onto a canoe and punch holes in it then left the canoe adrift in the open ocean. He would beat them with a club until they are dead, usually for very minor offenses. He would rage and rage over official appointments which did not please him....like the appointment of his first cousin Princess Tupou Moheofo as the 12th Tu'i Kanokupolu, sometime during the 'age' of Captain James Cook, who visited Tonga in 1773, 1774 and 1777. She was the daughter of Tupoulahimu'a, the 7th Tu'i Kanokupolu.

Tuku'aho, who was Governmor of 'Eua
Island decided to do something about it.
He believed his father Mumui, who is the
younger brother of Tupoulahimu'a (TK7)
should be appointed king and not Tupou
Moheofo, who is a daughter of
Tupoulahimu'a. Tuku'aho raised an
army and attacked Tupou Moheofo's
supporters in central Tongatapu and
won. Tupou Moheofo and a few warriors
escaped to the Ha'apai Group where
Tuku'aho caught up with them. Tupou
Moheofo had raised an army from her
relatives in Ha'apai. The Tu'i Ha'apai,
Ngalumoetutulu being her uncle. He
being the eldest brother of
Tupoulahimu'a and Mumui.

The battle that followed was so fierce on
one of the island beaches, legend told of
the sea turning red with blood and the
beach later turned white with the bones
of the dead. Tupou Moheofo was, again,
defeated. She escaped to the Vava'u
Island Group to seek refuge with her

nephew the Tu'i Vava'u, Finau 'Uluakalala II. He was the grandson of the Tu'i Ha'apai, Ngalumoetutulu. 'Ulukalala II, also known as 'Ulukalala 'i Feletoa.

He was a strong king and Tuku'aho did not dare to attack his fortress, he was just a Governor not a king. The Vava'u Islands were united under 'Ulukalala and it is a very large group of islands reputed to be even stronger than the kings of Tongatapu.

'Ulukalala II, whose mother 'Ulukilupetea, daughter of Ngalumoetutulu, is Tupoumoheofo's first cousin, was obligated to defend and look after his elderly aunt. She was also of very high rank being the great grand-daughter of the 32nd Tu'i Tonga Uluakimata II, on her mother's side. The Tu'i Tonga being the most paramount chief in all the country.

Tuku'aho, who was only a Governor, was

of very low rank and had no business raging war against her, an appointed King of much higher rank. The people of Ha'apai, Vava'u, and 'Ulukalala's relatives were angered by Tuku'aho's behavior.

However, Tuku'aho did appoint his father, Mumui, who is Tupoumoheofo's uncle, to be the 13th Tu'i Kanokupolu, sometime in the early 1790s, after it became apparent he had defeated Tupou Moheofo. Mumui is the younger brother of Tupoulahimu'a, Tupou Moheofo's father. It became obvious that Tuku'aho's actions in Ha'apai against Tupou Moheofo had turned a lot of chiefs against him. In particular Maealiuaki second brother to Ngalumoetutulu who was the 8th Tu'i Ha'a Takalaua and 15th Tu'i Kanokupolu. Maealiuaki was also an older brother of Mumui.

Tupou Moheofo was the Principal Wife of Pau the 36th Tu'i Tonga, who

4

entertained Captain James Cook with such hospitality that Captain James Cook called the islands 'The Friendly Islands'. Fatafehi Fuanunu'iava, the only son of Pau and Tupou Moheofo, was only 12 years old when Cook visited in 1777. Tupou Moheofo's son with Pau, Fatafehi Fuanunu'iava, succeeded to the throne as the 38th Tu'i Tonga and his son Laufilitonga, who became the 39th Tu'i Tonga was born in 1797 and died in 1865.

It came to pass that Tuku'aho succeeded his father as the 14th Tu'i Kanokupolu, with his resident at Mu'a, the capital, and thereby sealed his fate. When an opportunity arose during a family gathering at Tongatapu in 1799, 'Ulukalala and his relatives and supporters arranged for the Palace Guards at Mu'a, to be replaced by their own, with the blessings of Maealiuaki. William Mariner, in his book, Tonga Islands described the assassination.....
The Vava'u Warriors had appointed one

of their own, Tupouniua, a half-brother of 'Ulukalala II to do the assassination. He entered the Palace grounds at night with an iron axe and he woke Tuku'aho with a slap to the face and said, "Tuku'aho, it is I Tupouniua that strikes"...and he smashed him on the head with the iron axe, so hard, it killed him instantly.

It also became apparent that Maealiuaki, older brother of Mumui and younger brother of Tupoulahimu'a, who approved of the assassination....is now the heir to the throne. He had resigned as Tu'i Ha'a Takalaua to become the 15th Tu'i Kanokupolu after the death of Tuku'aho.

It was Maealiuaki's authority that helped to replace the Palace Guards and gave the warriors from Vava'u a free hand in the assassination.

Many of the supporters of Tuku'aho did not like what happened, in particular, his son Tupouto'a, who is also a younger son of 'Ulukilupetea.

 The civil war raged until 1852 , the winning side led by Taufa'ahau established a new Government in 1875, ten years after the death of the 39th Tu'i Tonga Laufilitonga. Although there were many Chiefs in the country only 20 were selected in the new Government. Later another 13 were appointed to make a total of 33 nobles. The rest of the Chiefs....mostly on the losing side of the civil war....were not appointed.

One of the problems after the civil war was the question of the 39th Tu'i Tonga, Laufilitonga. He had led the losing side and although he lost in battle in 1827 he was still allowed to continue until his death in 1865.

There were still pockets of resistance all over the country. It took another 20-30 years to bring them under Taufa'ahau's control. Taufa'ahau was Tuku'aho's

grandson, being the son of Tupouto'a
and Taufa Hoamofaleono.

Even after the death of the Tu'i Tonga, it
was still difficult for the country to come
to terms with the new management,
after 900 or so years of Tu'i Tonga rule.
It took another 10 years of negotiations
before everyone agreed to form a
Government in the Westminister model,
with the help of the British Missionaries.
It was the only way forward, as
Taufa'ahau did not have the high rank
necessary to make him king in the
ancient Tongan hierarchy.

The learned missionaries from England,
in Tonga at the time, helped to set up
the new Government with a Constitution.
The most influential being the Reverend
Shirley Baker who also became the
Prime Minister.

One of the most important laws under
the new Constitution was that all male
Tongans will be given a town allotment
of 30 poles and a tax allotment of 81/4

acres, upon reaching the age of 16. This was totally new as communal ownership was the norm...but more likely...everything belongs to the Chiefs who will decide whether to share them or not.

Taufa'ahau also took on the title King George Tupou I, after King George of England, when he became a Christian.

"Wow, this is fantastic Grandpa. Where did you get this information from?", George said enthusiastically as he glanced up from the photocopied yellowing A4 pages.

"I found them in my Grandmother's stuff which no one wanted. So I kept them for many years, then one day I decided to go through them and found that file. It was written by a journalist from England...or somebody like that and....I guess forgotten. You can see they are turning yellow with age". Grandfather William looked out the window at the rain outside...his mind going back many years. His grandmother, Maryanne, still fresh in his memory. She was a scholar in the early days of education, although limited. He used to visit her as a kid but does not remember much. His memory not as sharp as it used to be. His 75 year old body shaking a bit as he tries to get up.

"I want you to go through all those writings and tell me what's in them. I did not get to read all of them. I just put them in a box and saved them to read someday and never got around to it". Grandpa William got up, shaking as usual. He got his walking stick and proceeded towards the kitchen.

"It might keep you busy during this rain. They usually last for a week or two. Normal weather in March", he said as he turned on the electric jug in the kitchen to make a cup of tea.

George was studying at the University

of Auckland and normally comes to Tonga during the school holidays. He had been lucky in the last 2 years. He won a scholarship from the New Zealand Government to do his PhD, studying Pacific history and doing archaeology as a hobby. Previously he was a private student, paying his way from part-time jobs and summer vacation work. He had planned to return to Auckland at the end of February but decided to stay another month and go through his grandfather's records and files. It might come in useful with his PhD research on Pacific history. It certainly has a lot of information on the early days of the Tongan Government.

"Hi George!, you are up early", his Grandmother Mary Latu said as she came out of their bedroom, smiling widely and kissed George on the cheek. "Did Grandpa bore you with his history stories?".

"No Grandma, it is actually very

interesting. I think it will come in useful with my studies", George said as he hugged his frail Grandmother who gave him a pat on the head.

"I have the jug ready for a cup of tea, Mary. Come and have a cuppa with me and George", William said as he poked his head out the kitchen door.

They never call each other pet names, darling, honey and all the other cooey stuff. His Grandparents always address each other by their first names. They live by themselves in a little 2 bedroom bungalow in a suburb of Nuku'alofa called Longolongo. According to legend, the whole area was covered with Longolongo palms, a member of the cycad family, before people moved in; hence the name. Much of the area is still covered in swamps, which is probably why cycads were growing there in abundance. They do well in waterlogged and wet areas.

George was reading through a

document... listen to this "Latu was a Chief of the village of Falehau in Niuatoputapu. Is that where you got the name Latu from?".

" I think so. The Chiefs of Niuatoputapu were addressed as Latu similar to Fiji where they call their Chiefs Ratu. They were two brothers, grandsons of the Tu'i Lakepa, who was a Fijian named Tapu'osi, with Princess Sinaitakala'ilangileka. One brother Latu Mailangi became Governor of Niuatoputapu. He met the Dutch explorers Schouten and Lemaire in 1616. He is the ancestor of the Ma'atu Chiefly family. Now known as Lord Ma'atu. The other brother Latu Nautu stayed behind at Mu'a. His descendants are still there to-day".

William came in and sat down, shakily on his favourite chair, a present from George when he came last time. It was a special in a store at Kingsland, Auckland. A large well padded chair,

similar to a sofa. Suitable for an old
man to lounge on all day.

"Apparently, Latu Mailangi, became the
Chief or King of Niuatoputapu and he
ceded the island to Taufa'ahau in 1862.
He was appointed as one of the first 20
nobles in the Government of 1875.
They gave him the Noble title Ma'atu. It
was a British System with a Tongan
arrangement".

William was smiling and turned and
winked at Mary who was trying hard
not to laugh.

George kept on digging through the box
of papers and pulled out a document
with a plastic cover. It looks very new.

"This looks like a title to a property".
George laughed so loud and jumped up
and hugged both his Grandparents. The
name on the property is George Latu!

He opened the plastic cover. There
were two titles in it. One for a 30 pole

town allotment in Longolongo and another for an 81/4 acre piece of land in the Eastern Districts.

"Thanks Grandpa. Is that why you wanted me to go through this box of stuff?", George was still laughing.

"Yeah. I guess so. I thought you should have them, your Dad rang from Auckland and told me to do it. He gave me the authorization to pass them on to you. They are your heritage to pass on to your children", William smiled and George could almost detect a sense of pride in his voice.

"Manu is not returning to stay. He said you plan to return and work here for a while after you finish your PhD".

"Yes, that is the plan", George said thoughtfully. Already thinking, what to do with his new found assets.

Mary was wiping her eyes as George gave her a hug and kiss on the cheek.

She also got a lounge chair from him last Christmas.

"You are lucky George. Land is becoming scarce these days. Many young people do not inherit land anymore. That is probably why many move overseas. A lot of Tongan people with no land here have bought land for themselves in New Zealand, Australia and the United States ".

"Yes, I guess so. Tell me more about Latu. What happened to him after the island was ceded to Taufa'ahau?", George asked with keen interest.

"When the 20 nobles were selected in 1875 and the estates or land divided among them, many of the title holders before became redundant. The King added another 13 nobles about 10 years later and that is how it stood to this day", William explained peering out the window at the rain as it drizzles down.

"According to this record, all the land belong to the King who allocates them to the nobles as caretakers. The young men in the villages can apply for a town and tax allotment when they are 16 years old. The Ministry of Lands draw up the Deed and the Minister of Lands and Noble of the village signs it and that young man effectively owns that land and pass it on to his heirs. That is how it has worked in the past. The only limitation is that no one is allowed to sell their land but you can give your land as a gift to family members". William was looking at George, almost peering over the rim of his glasses.

"And what do you intend to do with your land?".

"I think I will build a house on the town allotment and live there. Maybe start a farm on the tax allotment, Grandpa".

"That is a good plan. When your father left 25 years ago, he only had a 3 month

visa; but 25 years later he is still there",
Grandpa William was laughing.

"Yeah, I was too young to understand
what was going on. I was only 5 years
old", George said rather sheepishly.

"I kept calling him and telling him to
come back but he kept saying he has an
opportunity to bring the family to New
Zealand and it went on and on for
months", Mary said wiping her eyes.

Manu, George's father, went on a work
visa to New Zealand in 1980 and
decided to stay. He worked at the
freezing works at Southdown and then
got married to a girl he met at a party.
It was a work programme started by a
relative to bring them to New Zealand
to earn a bit of capital to help build up
their lives. Many decided to stay and it
became a major immigration issue.

The islanders could not understand
why the New Zealand Government
cannot grant them residence since

their ancestors have been visiting New Zealand for hundreds of years. Many Polynesians believe that New Zealand is Hawaiki in their mythologies, although some say it is Hawaii...the ancestral home of the Polynesians.

There are many stories about Hawaiki...an island in the middle of the Pacific Ocean where the God Tangaroa met a mortal woman and beget the first Polynesian man.

Chapter Two....

MIGRATION

Manu looked outside the window as the plane approaches Auckland International Airport. He can feel the cold inside the plane. A stewardess gave him a blanket but he was still cold. It was sunny outside. He can see houses and buildings, looking like white match boxes below, stretching as far as he can see. Vehicles were running around on the road arteries...down below... like busy ants collecting food. The pilot announces they will be landing in 30 minutes. The stewardess came around with a basket of lollies. He took a whole handful. She smiled. "Maybe I am taking too many", he thought so he took two and put the rest back.

"Its alright, take them", she said with another smile.

"Wow! She is very pretty". Manu thought, feeling a bit ashamed of his apparent attraction to another woman. He knows Heilala does not like him talking about other women.

She sounded like his Physics teacher at Tonga High School. She was from New Zealand. His Science teacher was a Peace Corp volunteer from the United States and he sounded different. 'Accents'….he told Manu. "Americans have different accents from New Zealanders", Doug said when he asked him. "Something to do with Geographical locations", Doug theorized.

Manu took another two lollies, smiled then looked outside the window. The fields were passing as in a dream…as the plane descended, fields and more fields with cows and sheep…endless numbers of cows and sheep…the plane landed with a bump then roared briefly….rolling towards the other end of the runway. It turned and cruised back to the terminal.

Manu was thinking about the cows and sheep. He has not seen so many all at once! He stood up and picked up his bag from the overhead locker and followed the passengers. The plane was full so it was a bit crowed. It was cold outside as he entered the building, wondering how the cows and sheep can be so comfortable in the cold weather .The middle of winter, somebody said. It was mid-July.

He didn't know where to go so he just followed everyone to check out at immigration and customs. Finally after queuing for half an hour and getting his passport stamped, he went outside. It was surprisingly warm in the arrival reception area. His cousin Tu'uta was waiting with a Maori man, who had a tattoo on his face. Tu'uta was waving enthusiastically.

" Hi, there cuz. It's been a long time".

"Yeah", Tu'uta smiled and hugged Manu then introduced Wayne. "This is Wayne. We work at Southdown freezing works. The tattoo on his face is called a moko".

"Kia ora bro", Wayne said as he gave Manu a hongi and a hug. "Welcome to Aotearoa". Wayne had a big smile on his face. He looked more like a warrior. Manu thought, with his shoulder long hair, tattooed face and hands and jean outfit. He reminds Manu of his grandfather. A very tough and hard working man.

 Manu was smiling like he wanted to jump with joy. 'Nice to meet you Wayne', he managed to say in a formal way. He was brought up to show respect to his elders and leaders. He felt that Wayne is going to be his leader in the next few months.

"Come let's talk on the way to the car. The boys are roasting a pig at our flat....we also have a few beers in the car", Tu'uta smiled…then laughed…. "the usual stuff!".

"Sounds good bro", Manu said with a wide grin, almost laughing. He hasn't had any beer since he got married a few years ago. He used to enjoy sharing a few drinks with the boys, but Heilala had put a stop to his drinking...and there was no one to share his drinks with.

Tu'uta and some of the Tongan men employed at Southdown freezing works were flatting together in a three bedroom flat at Kingsland, near Morningside. There were six of them with Wayne. Wayne acts as an interpreter and also help to fill any paper work they need done. He was a very good mate, according to them.

"So how did you get involved in the work scheme Manu?", Wayne asked.

"Oh, I was told by a man in our village. A cousin was married to one of the

Managers at Southdown and she asked him to arrange for her relatives to come and work there for some extra money. They heard of a similar scheme they were doing at the Royal Easter Show at Epsom".

"So you are also Marian's relative?", Wayne asked.

"Yes, we are all in the same group". Wayne understood the strong and close bond between the men, they are all cousins or uncles. He was looking outside the car window too, thinking of his whanau up north.

The food was ready when they arrived. A roasted suckling pig, 'umu roasted yams, taro and cassava with mussels, octopus in coconut cream and raw fish. Manu was hungry after drinking two large bottles of DB Brown on the way, while he tries not to breath in the exhaust fumes which seems to come out of the floor!. Tu'uta's red Ford Cortina was probably older than

Noah's Ark, as Wayne puts it.

After the usual greetings and hugging, 'Aisea, the oldest man in the group said grace. It turned out to be a half hour prayer, which everyone in the group are used to. He was very tearful, as were the other men. Manu is used to it at his local Free Wesleyan Church in Tonga. The long prayers, the tearful confessions and speeches.

They were all blood related and it is a very strong bond in the Tongan culture. 'Aisea gave a speech and talked about why they are in New Zealand….to make some money for their families. Some of the men want to build a house….others want to buy a car or van to take back to Tonga. They were all farmers and a one or two tonne hiace van or truck is considered a better transport option than the current horse and cart used universally in Tonga.

"I really love this island food, man.

Can't get enough of it", Wayne laughed as he stood up and helped himself to the food on the table after 'Aisea's prayer and speech. Wayne was always the guest of honor at their gatherings and he rather like his special status. "I usually have seconds and thirds, especially the crackling suckling pig man…that's divine", he joked to Manu who was the next on the guest list and standing beside him at the table as they piled up the food on the plates. Wayne and Manu sat down on the large and only sofa in the living room and talked. Manu couldn't help noticing the peeling paint on the ceiling and window sills. He will definitely paint the house as soon as he gets some money, he thought.

The others were sitting on wooden chairs and even a wooden beer crate. Wayne went on to talk about his family. He is from up north. A place called Whangarei. He only comes down for work and usually goes back to Whangarei for long weekends. Manu talked about his dream of bringing his family to New Zealand but he doesn't know how. Wayne explained to him he has to apply to the Immigration Department for permanent residence. Once he's got that then he can apply for citizenship about three years later if he wants to.

"That'll be good, if I can get permanent residence". Manu was looking hopeful, taking a long swig from the bottles of DB Brown that Tu'uta handed them. The living room was getting a bit crowded and noisy.

"Yeah, I have a cousin who is a lawyer….I will get her to talk to you next week…if you want", Wayne offered almost shouting above the noise.

"Thanks". Manu was really keen, even before he started working. He will join them at Southdown on Monday.

Some of the men prefer to drink a few

more beers before eating. Then Wayne brought out his guitar and started singing Pokarekareana...they all joined in. Manu thought they must have had plenty of practice. Sounds like a Choir!. They kept on singing long into the night after the food was finished and more beer appeared.

On Monday, they all trooped into Tu'uta's and two other cars and shot off early to Southdown freezing works. It was all new to Manu...he had never seen such a large building in his whole life. The roads were all smooth and clean and street lights were amazing. Not a single pot hole anywhere. He is used to the large pot holes on the roads at Nuku'alofa and other villages on Tongatapu, some as a big as a car!

He was shown the ropes and he learned quickly....boning, skinning and many other skills. Every Friday, they would have a few beers in the canteen. Wayne will bring his guitar and sing a few songs. Manu was always careful to put his money in the bank as soon as he gets it on Thursday afternoon. Wayne had helped him open a bank account at the local Auckland Savings Bank Branch. He always donates $10 for the beer rounds and $40 towards the rent and shopping, every week. He puts the rest…about $100 in the bank. He figures he will have $1200 by the time his visa expires. They told him he can renew for a further three months and that's it.

He thinks of his wife and four kids every night. He did not realize he will miss them at all! But he did….and one night while drunk from the usual Friday beer rounds he cried outside in the garden….'Aisea realized Manu was missing and went looking outside and he could hear the faint sobbing from under a feijoa tree at the back of the yard.

He went over and sat down beside Manu. He knows the feeling…he has been away from his own family for five months…and he did not realize how terrible it feels sometimes…missing the familiar sounds of the kids playing outside and his wife lying beside him…the smell of her candle nut perfume that she use to rub her skin before her evening bath…he too also cried many times in the back garden….usually after a heavy bout of drinking.

"I know the feeling, Manu. I too also cried here many times before. But I am getting used to it and looking forward to going back home next month", 'Aisea put his arms around Manu and took a swig from his bottle of DB Brown. Manu just continued sobbing on his shoulders.

'Aisea went back inside and got Manu a bottle and they sat drinking and talking outside, then fell asleep under the tree; listening to Wayne and the boys singing Pokarekareana from inside. They later woke up and went back inside, shaking from the cold. It's a good thing they have thick jackets on Aisea pointed out.

Manu felt better in the following weeks knowing that it is normal to have a cry….when he misses all those things that he loves. The sound of tiny feet on the concrete in their little house. The kids playing in the morning and shouting at each other when he wakes up. His wife…the familiar sounds and smells, but he was determined to stay six months so he can get at least $2,000 saved. It might be enough for a van so he can take his produce to Talamahu Market in Nuku'alofa. Some of the bigger growers in the village boasted they can make $1,000 a week in the market…but they have trucks, tractors and workers to do everything and sell their produce in town almost every day.

A few months later, Wayne invited everyone over to Whangarei for his birthday. He wants to have a hangi with his family and he and the boys can blow the candles, share the cake and sing happy birthday. He only has a brother and his parents left. There were two other brothers who moved to Australia after disputes…almost every day…with their Mrs… as they call their wives. It was becoming a national solution to argumentative couples…for one of them to move to Australia,Wayne used to joke.

The Whangarei party was a huge one! There was a pig on the spit, a steer was slaughtered and half was cooked in a boil-up….a rather large pot with kumara, puha, watercress and some spice, the rest of the steer was butchered and put in the hangi with more kumara, chicken and other delicacies in pots. Stacks of beer crates were on the lawn. The usual favorites DB Brown and Lion Red. Heaps of small canned beer in a bath tub full of ice with the usual 750 ml bottles. Manu thought there might be at least 50 people there, all standing around the back lawn. The house was a typical four bedroom Victorian wooden house seen in many homes around Auckland.

After the cake ceremony, they sang happy birthday to Wayne, who was clapping and laughing. He was looking very happy. There were speeches from Wayne and his parents and relatives, then the Tongan boys sang "Silent Night"…in Tongan with some Tongan carols….all hymns…in their Free Wesleyan Church…Everyone were so quiet as they listened to the boys sing…they have never heard such beautiful foreign songs before…and they know the tunes. They sang along to "Silent Night" in English as the boys sang in Tongan

…."Po Malu….Ko Si'i Po….Hifo ai e 'Alo….Mele mo Siosifa…na'ana maata….fanautama …'a..Tangata..ko…si'ene totofaa"…

A young Maori woman, who was a bit drunk, came and put some money on Manu…as they have seen Wayne do with 'Aisea. He was standing at the back in the dark. Then she kissed him on the lips....Manu was also a bit drunk...he kissed her back. She grabbed his hand and led him behind the house as the boys finished off the song...with everyone...following in English. They did not even see the two of them disappear behind the bushes at the back. It was too dark, with just a large fire burning beside the hangi.

They were all shedding a few tears. It was just a month before Christmas...and they were all in the Christmas mood. They partied on until dawn...no one took notice of the goings on, of course, and they all disappear off into the night with female partners.

Wayne had to find all of them before Sunday night so they can head back to Auckland....to work on Monday. It was the beginning of many weekend parties at his parent's farm...and the end for most of the boy's marriages as they started to move in with their new girlfriends. Manu stayed with 'Aisea and Wayne…while the rest moved out. They all have one room each…but they still meet every Friday for a few drinks…with the girlfriends coming along…and the singing got louder and louder….usually ending with *Po Malu.*

That Christmas…they had a huge party. They invited many of their colleagues from Southdown after the Christmas party….Manu got a huge shock! His girlfriend Kiri was pregnant…and so were some of the other girls! But they were all too drunk to care…and a few joints of marijuana were also circulating. Manu had never smoked it before….and he got really sick after. He wasn't sure whether it was the marijuana or the beer. He was throwing up all over his girlfriend and the new lounge suites, they bought for Christmas. Everyone just laughed and pointed at him as the stereo blasted its way all the way down the street….while everyone were dirty dancing the night away. The whole house was full of smoke and people....it stank of marijuana for a long...long time after. Steven used to joke...that's why the paint inside and outside their greyish coloured flat are peeling!

There were a few suckling pigs, the usual raw fish and octopus with yams, taro and cassava on the table in the living room. There were watermelons from Australia as well as watercress, puha and kumara. Kiri tried to get Manu to eat something. "It will sober you up"...she says.."and drink this coffee sweetie". Heilala never called him sweetie or anything other than plain old Manu...so it kind of flattered him when Kiri calls him darling, honey or sweetie. He knew he was getting soft.

After eating, Kiri led Manu to their room...with a cold towel on his head...after the nth cup of iced tea. She bathed him with warm water and fragrant oil and gave him a "body massage"…it was the first of many during those Christmas holidays. They can barely hear the noise as Kiri put some towels under the door.

They slept like babies that night.

Manu had begun to forget his family…he did not even bother to send money that Christmas. Only 'Aisea sent money to his wife…like he always did the whole 10 months before and he hasn't got a girlfriend yet. He was a lay preacher in their local Church and it was taboo…for him to even look at another woman…even though he has a few beers with the boys. All the rest were thinking of staying and never returning back to Tonga. Their new girlfriends were just too sweet, kind and loved them to bits….and they were all pregnant!

They all decided to attend the local Tongan Methodist Church that New Year's Eve. Usually there were twelve or so sermons…with twelve feasts for each of those lay preachers or Church Ministers. The Church Steward invited them to one of the feasts in the afternoon…with their girlfriends…which was the source of local gossip. Their girlfriends were really impressed with the Tongan style feasts…just about all kinds of foods in the Auckland markets were in it…all piled high on the table…covered in aluminium foil. Bottles of sparkling juice and fruits lining the sides. The only thing missing was alcohol, the consumption of which was not allowed in the Methodist Church. A row of roast suckling pigs in the middle of the table. The smell of the cooked roast pigs just waters their mouths. It's a kind of Tongan delicacy, no feast is complete without the roast suckling pigs. The Church Hall where the feast was held was also decorated with balloons and flowers to give it a festive atmosphere.

They young men were thinking….about settling

down…joining the Church and divorcing their wives. This is the kind of life they only dream about in the islands.

Kiri felt a bit sick during the feast and had to go to the toilet…she feels she might throw up. She was pregnant but the tell tale lump hasn't showed up yet. Manu was really surprised… at how much he cared for her…he immediately got up and followed her to the bathroom…..with the church women staring after him. It was a large hall and he can feel the eyes on his back, a kind of shame mixed with love for Kiri was creeping in misting his eyes as he walked after her. He knows he loves her and the baby and would do anything for them.

That night when the sermon started…the Church Minister, the Reverend Finau Valevale invited all the "Tongan Boys" from Southdown to the front and introduced them to the congregation. 'Aisea…who was usually keen to sing…volunteered they will sing *Po Malu* for them…and they did. Many of the older women wiped their eyes. Those young men under 'Aisea's care…who have strayed from the fold…can sing so beautifully…like most of the Wesleyan youth….even their girlfriends cried. They realize how much it means to them…to be in church...singing and…probably thinking of their families in the islands this New Year's Eve.

At 12 am…they played a tape recorder with a message from the President of the Church wishing everyone a happy new year….then there was a lot of kissing and hugging…before they all went back to the flat. No one wanted to drink so they just crashed in the lounge. The girlfriends, blanket and a sheet to keep them warm until dawn.

Chapter Three....

THE CHURCH

In 1980 there were 13 Tongan Methodist congregations in Auckland or were in the process of being established. The Church membership went through the roof as the Sunday...and even the Wednesday services...were full of people. Many of them have never been to church for a long time...and some had spent most weekends in the pubs. Many gave up the bottle in favour of the gospel....and so did Manu and his mates from Southdown. 'Aisea had returned to Tonga...he had worked some extra months...but did not want to stay. Now they start to have regular bible evenings and legal counselling on divorce proceedings and getting married to their girlfriends in Auckland.

It wasn't painful to think of their

families anymore…they were just kind of…indifferent. They wrote to their wives and advise them to find a new partner and move on…as they will not be coming back…. enclosing the divorce papers.

Kiri was very pleased that Manu has been very open with her. He had told her about his family and his dreams. Now…he tells her he is divorcing his wife. She plans to take him up north to meet her family once they are married.

The Kingsland Tongan Methodist Church was just one hundred metres down New North Road from where the flat was. Manu began to attend Church regularly…he also asked the Church Minister to make him a lay preacher and started weekly training with some of the other men from Church.

Only Manu and Wayne and their girlfriends were still left in the flat, although they still have their Friday parties. Manu has given up beer in favour of orange juice….and the bible…he is now a "trainee" lay preacher, he says. The boys thought it was a bit of a joke, but slowly realize he is really serious. Pictures of Jesus began to appear on the walls of the flat. He bought some paint and painted the rooms and living room white. A little altar was setup with tapa cloth in one corner…then there were wall hangers of famous hymns like "Nearer my God to thee".

One Friday, Manu started singing the Tongan version of the hymn "Nearer my God to thee"….."*Kehe keu ofi pe kiate koe*"…the boys were a bit drunk and they all wept….feeling like real sinners for the first time. Wayne too did not feel like singing his usual songs anymore or playing the guitar…he decided to learn Tongan and attend Church too. He simply loved being with the Tongan boys and sharing in their culture.

Kiri's tummy was getting bigger and

the Church women were getting a bit jealous. They now know Manu is divorcing his wife he is marrying Kiri and becoming a lay preacher in their Church. Manu was in his 30s, so he was still young. He was good looking, tall and well build…and even some of the young girls in Church fancied him when they first attended Sunday service.

One of the men made it a point in his sermon that Sunday…. "that all have sinned in the eyes of God….but if you repent your sins and ask for forgiveness….he will wash away your sins with his blood….and you will be whiter than snow". Snow and white… being a reference to cleanliness of the soul. Probably a metaphor of the….pure in heart…like the parable on the Mount. "Blessed are the pure in heart for they shall inherit the Kingdom of Heaven"…he says.

Wayne was really intrigued with the teachings of the bible. He had never been a Church goer…although he attended Church with his grandparents as a child…but he stopped going to Church a long time ago. They often talk late into the night with Manu about his bible lessons. Manu's English was really good and he could carry on a conversation about abstract ideas and bible themes with Wayne…although he had a heavy Tongan accent.

"Do you think they will let me be a lay preacher in the Church, Manu?", Wayne asked one day.

"Yeah…if you can speak Tongan fluently and attend the bible lessons…I am sure the Minister will appoint you to be a lay preacher".

Manu and Wayne started attending the bible lessons each week. Wayne's Tongan was improving after two weeks. "It's easy for me…Tongan is very similar to Maori, "fale" in Tongan is "whare" in Maori…the pronounciation is the same although f is replaced by wh, "fakafiefia" is

"whakawhiewhia"…other words
include mokopuna…kaumatu'a and so
on…Wayne explained…but was
surprised at the similarities.

After one month…the Minister…the
most Reverend Finau Valevale
announced they were to have a test the
next Wednesday evening at Dominion
Road Methodist Church. Lay preacher's
usually have several "practice runs" on
Wednesday nights before they are
allowed to preach on Sundays.

Even Kiri was interested in learning
Tongan….she has started speaking to
Manu in Tongan….which was always a
source of laughter for him. "How are
you my darling" was translated to "*Fefe
hake fo'ilole?*"…..that came from
Sitiveni…one of their mates from
Southdown. She asked Wayne… "Why
is Manu always laughing when I say
"*Fefe hake fo'i lole?*". Wayne
translated…that literally means "How
are you sweet lolly?". Kiri laughed till
her stomach was sore… "I am going to

wring Sitiveni's neck", she laughed.

Kiri was in her late twenties. She was a really beautiful girl. Slender, light brown skin and eyes. White straight teeth and a ready smile. Long black hair down to her waist. She used to smoke pot but gave up when she got pregnant…she was stoned that first night when she kissed Manu on the lips at Wayne's birthday party. But she was glad…because Manu turned out to be a gentleman…a bit rough on the edges….like Maori men…but very gentle with her. She was already planning their wedding. She wants to show off her man to her relatives up north to show them how proud she is of him.

Manu's 3 months was over. The Immigration Department gave him another 3 month's work visa. A letter of recommendation from the Southdown management decided the issue. He was a hard worker and held in high regard by his workmates.

The legal counsellor told him he needs to hurry things up if he wants to get it done within the next 2 months…That is divorce then get married. He might not get a third 3 month's visa from immigration as they normally only grant 6 month's work visa.

Manu filled in the forms then posted them to his wife.

They have a little brick house with concrete floor at Pahu…a suburb of Nuku'alofa. It only had two rooms…one bedroom and a living room…doubling as kitchen when it rains. They have a kerosene stove in one corner. Heilala…Manu's wife.. got his letter from the Post Office. She had arranged with the Post Office workers to call her if she has a letter. It was her cousin who usually calls.

Heilala was very happy. She had not received a letter from Manu in almost two months. She has a little money from her handicraft making which helps pay the bills and feed the kids, buy their uniforms, stationery and other necessities. Manu used to send $100 a month, which was a large amount. It paid for a lot of things.

She hurried home and opened the letter. It was some forms for her to sign and a letter from Manu saying…he wants a divorce…he met another woman in New Zealand. She could not hold back the tears as it ran down her cheeks…and she wailed like there was a funeral. The kids were at school….no one was home. She just curled up on the concrete floor in the middle of the kitchen and cried at the top of her voice. They have been talking about their future and how the van will solve a lot of problems especially his farming and transporting her handicrafts to town and the tourist sightseeing spots. She felt it was the end of her world….nothing seems to matter to her anymore… after an hour of wailing at the top of her voice…it was so

hoarse…she just cried
silently…rocking back and forth on the
floor until the kids arrived home from
school.

Manu put on his best suit with a wrap
around tupenu…instead of pants. He
had been rehearsing for his first
sermon in the past week…getting
critiques from his Southdown mates,
Wayne and Kiri. She laughed when he
asked her to listen while he practise. "I
don't know most of the things you say
but I can tell you whether it sounds and
looks good", she giggled.

" 'E 'Eiki keke to'o ho mau loungutu"….

Manu sang out at the top of his
voice…the congregation erupted into a
powerful rendition…ending with the
lord's prayer. Wayne thought he had
never heard such powerful
singing…before. "You know, it's like
people singing with gusto", he says.

Manu talked about the prodigal son in

his sermon and the power of forgiveness to restore the *mana* of the son…after he apologised for leaving and squandering the family fortune. He had heard of the word *mana* from Wayne and he thought it is a good word to use to describe the dignity of a person…but much, much more. Mana brings together all that is good about a person in terms of his community and family. The respect they have for him…his dignity and leadership qualities and so on.

He suddenly remembered his oldest son George running away one Saturday morning with some kids to swim and fish at the wharf. He did not come home until about 8 o'clock at night. Manu was inside listening to the transistor radio…and he heard Heilala giving George the rules in very strict language…even slapping him on the ears for going out that long and not even asking for permission. He was about 5 at the time, just a month before Manu left. He got George to come and lay down beside him so they can talk about his day and why he was away from home for that long. Manu did learn a few things about how his 5 year old son thinks.

He wept on the pulpit. Not trusting himself to say something or he might start talking about things he will regret later. After a few seconds of silence he pulled himself together…wiped his eyes with his handkerchief. Kiri wanted to go up and hug him and try his tears. It occurred to her that maybe he is thinking of his own son…while he was talking about the parable of the prodigal son.

Manu finished off his sermon….with the Tongan version of "Nearer my God to Thee"…one of his favourite hymns…the whole congregation were in tears. They all understood why he is crying…they all know about his 5 year old son George. Many of the men had also left their families in Tonga and married a woman in Auckland…they too cried for their sons that night. The hymn was very comforting…and perhaps…they think it is the main reason why most of them come to Church to seek solace…or forgiveness that only God can give them. It keeps them from feeling guilty about leaving and falling apart or worse…..soul destroying guilt.

After the last sermon…the Minister gave a speech and congratulated the 5 men who were tested that night. They will now receive Sunday sermons in the next calendar year of the Church.

Chapter 4....

THE WEDDING

Manu had received the forms back from Heilala. There were ink blotches all over it. The lawyer said it looks like tears causing the ink blotches on the form. Manu also felt emotional himself. Everything was in order, the divorce was official as soon the officials are informed. Manu and Kiri planned to marry that weekend on a private farm in Whangarei belonging to her family. Manu did not have any relatives to come to the wedding…only his mates from Southdown freezing works, about 30 of them! They plan to sing a few Tongan songs and do a *haka* to honour their mate's wedding . There were about 10 Tongan boys, the rest were Maori, Samoan, Niuean, Rarotongan and some Pakeha boys….as Wayne refers to the "*palangi* boys". That was the Tongan word for "Europeans"… *"palangi"*. Wayne had arranged a bus for them to go to the wedding together in the morning. It was only an hour's drive from Auckland to Whangarei, after the wedding they can drive back in the evening.

It was much larger than Manu thought...there were 3 marquees on one of the paddocks nearest the farmhouse. A large one and two smaller ones. The paddock must be 4 acres in size and the large marquee probably covered a whole acre!

The two smaller ones were for the food and the drinks. It was a buffet with self-service bars. Any beer or spirits available on the market was there, just help yourself to a beer or mix your drinks, they tell everyone....the food included a whole roasted steer, several roasted pigs and lambs and heaps of Maori seafood like *kina*, *paua* and other shellfish. Also octopus and raw fish. Manu had brought some yams, taro and cassava for the Maori hangi...heaps of kumara and potato salads, chips, fruits

as well. It was a typical mix of Pacific Island, Maori and Pakeha foods.
Manu had put on a Tongan suit with fine mats wrapped around him. A typical Tongan wedding attire. Kiri had a dress especially made because her stomach was starting to show. It was a loose white wedding dress with a Maori cloak on her shoulders, feathers on her hair and an artist even added a *moko* on her chin with felt pens! It was a nice touch. She looked stunning. Manu was so proud to watch her slow walk with her Dad to the front as they play Mendelssohn's wedding march. There must have been over 100 guests there. Relatives and friends and the Kingsland Tongan Methodist Church Choir! About 20 of them! The marquee was almost full of people.

The wedding was a simple ceremony. They read pledges to each other of love and faithfulness for the rest of their lives…in Tongan, Maori and English.

The Choir sang a hymn after each step

in English and Tongan…the crowd sang along to the bits they know.

Then the Minister of the Tongan Methodist Church, Reverend Finau Valevale, read from the bible and gave a short sermon…blessing the couple and their future.

Then the official bit, done by a Maori Wedding Celebrant…signing the papers…. and announcing of "man and wife". They kissed while everyone clapped, cheered and cat called.

A DJ started playing requested music….the bar was open and the food will be ready in an hour. One happy hour….Manu laughed as he toasted with Kiri with some sparkling juice. He did not even feel like he needed any alcohol. It really surprised him…as he usually feels like having a few beers at weddings. He looked at her radiant face and thought how lucky he is to have met this woman…who seem to fill his whole world like no one had ever done before. She smiled up at him then stood on her toes and kissed him on the lips…"I am lucky too, my darling", she smiled. She must have read my thoughts…he smiled…as the guests started coming to chat.

The Minister came and shook their hands and handed Manu an envelope. "This is a small gift from the Tongan Methodist Congregation at Kingsland. It will help you and Kiri start your new life".

Manu opened it. It was a large card signed by all the Church Members and a cheque for $ 1,000. They were both surprised and thanked the Minister as more and more guests come by with envelopes and gave them to Manu. Kiri understood, it was their Tongan custom to give money to the groom or bride to help them with getting started…to buy furniture and so on. At the end of the evening…they had more than $7,000 in cash and cheques. Kiri was very impressed with the Tongan congregation and Manu's mates…they are a very good bunch indeed. The baby would certainly need lots of stuff like cots, clothes and so on. They will also need a car.

There were also presents piled high on the designated table…and more envelopes.

The party was in full swing as the food bar opens and guests were enjoying themselves…laughing loudly… as they do in the islands.

Manu had given all his savings of $1,500 to Kiri to help pay for the costs…many of the food and drinks were also brought by family and friends. They were very happy as things turned out really well. They escaped into one corner as more and more dancers took up the middle of the marquee…and sat on a couch facing the paddock. Cows were crazing as the sun went down over the wooded hills at the farm boundary.

"It must be around 8 pm", Kiri said as she kissed him on the lips…putting one leg over his. They were silent for awhile…. "It's a good thing we don't drink alcohol anymore", she smiled….almost giggling…Manu nodded, as a noisy Wayne and some of their mates arrived and sang….Po Malu and Silent Night at the top of their voices…the DJ turned off the music and the lights except the candles…the moon was up and it was an eerie feeling….in the silence. Everybody stopped and listened….to hear that song "Silent Night" in a different language….in Maori country. "It almost sounds like Maori"….Kiri whispered to Manu. He was looking out over the paddock at the cows grazing in the moonlight and thought of a similar Christmas a long time ago when his parents took him to their farm to spend the holidays.

"Yeah…", he whispered…suddenly aware of her perfume as she put her head on his shoulder. The boys have practiced for a while they sound like a professional group. Everyone clapped when they finished the song.

Chapter Five....

DAWN RAID

A month later, Manu had lodged an application for permanent residence. Some of the boys at Southdown had left and returned to Tonga while others left and worked in farms. Their visa had expired and they were overstayers. Manu heard their relatives convinced them to stay and try and get their PR...then bring their families to New Zealand. His legal counsellor, Wayne's cousin, only shook her head. "It is the worst thing to do. You cannot overstay your visa then try to bring your family over". But she admits that some people have done so before and it worked...after 10 years or so... "too much of a sacrifice"...she said.

One early morning at about 5 there were loud knocks on their door. Wayne opened the door....there was an Immigration Officer with several Police

Officers outside…they were looking for Steven! Sitiveni..as Manu calls him…has decided to move to Pukekohe and work in a farm with an uncle….after 10 years or when there is an amnesty….he will get his PR and bring his family. Not the best plan but it has worked for some people.

"No, Sitiveni is no longer residing at this address. He has moved…I am not sure where", Wayne answered
"What nationality are you?", they asked.
"I am Maori. Can't you see the moko, bro?". Wayne said, a bit annoyed.
"Are there any Pacific Islanders residing at this address?", the Officer asked.
"Yes, just my mate and his Maori wife", Wayne answered.
"Can we speak to him?", the Officer insisted.
"What?, you don't believe me?", Wayne raised his voice to show his disapproval.

"Please?", the Officer said. "We just need to make sure that Mr Lemoto is not here".

"Who is that?", Wayne asked suspiciously.

"That is Sitiveni's surname", the Officer replied.

"Alright come into the lounge I will wake up Manu and his wife to come and talk to you". Wayne led them into the lounge and turned on the light. Wayne knocked on the door. Kiri and Manu were already up and putting on their clothes. They heard everything. They came into the living room.

"Can we ask you some questions?", the Officer asked Manu.

"Yes...sure".

"What is your full name?".

"Manu Latu".

"Where are you from...what is your nationality on your passport?".

"Tongan".

"Do you have a visa to be in this country?".

"Yes".

"Have you any identification to prove

who you are ?".

 "Yes, I have a passport".

"Can I have a look?", the Officer continued.

Manu, went into the room and got his passport.

After looking at his passport...Manu has a 3 months visa extension on it. He gave the passport back to Manu.

They wanted to have a look around the property. Wayne told them to go ahead. After an hour of poking around the bushes and trees outside, they had a quick look around the house and attic.

"Sorry to have bothered you"...the Officer told them and they all left single file through the door .

"Man...Sitiveni is such an idiot...that is not the best way to get your PR is to run away from the Immigration people!", Kiri was fuming. "He is such a nice person...but I think that was the wrong thing to do", she burst out to Manu and Wayne. They understood...she was always laughing at Steven's idiotic jokes!

"Sorry hon", she rubbed Manu's hand

then started making some coffee as the jug boiled. "Wayne..do you want a cup of coffee?".

"Sure, Kiri…Thanks".

They drank their coffee on the back porch and watch the mist lift off the grass. It was still early morning…but they can't go back to sleep.

"I hope Sitiveni is lucky with his PR plan", Kiri said seriously to Manu and Wayne.

"We can only hope I suppose", Wayne said seriously.

"Yeah…I hope so", Manu said… making an effort to say something.

Manu and Wayne got up and made some lunch to take with them to work. Kiri usually makes their lunch but they told her to enjoy her coffee while they do it. Manu came out on the porch again and gave his wife a big hug and kiss then they went out with Wayne in his new car. He bought a Ford Escort for $4,000. It was still in very good condition. He had also got a drivers licence with his Tongan Drivers Licence.

Kiri was very proud of their new car. It was probably 10-15 years old but still "new" to them.

"Tu'uta would have been very proud of you", Kiri had told him.

"Yeah…I miss that bugger…he didn't have to go back for a funeral with one month to go on his visa. But then…some people put more importance on things like that", Manu said looking out the window. Kiri thought he might cry…but he just shook his head.

Chapter Six....

THE BABY

Kiri was noticeably tired when she moves around the house doing the house chores. As the months pass and her stomach got bigger she moved a little slower. She seems to be easily irritated with little things that bother her.

One day when they were doing their shopping at the Foodtown Supermarket on Dominion Road...the checkout girl put in some of the groceries twice. It was only when Kiri noticed that she tried to correct it. She was not trying to cheat them but the mistake irritated her and she told the girl off. It surprised Manu...and he whispered in her ear... "Not too loud, darling"...and he laughed.

"Awww..sorry, honey"...was Kiri's usual response. She has that effect on him when she calls him those lovey-dovey names. He just melts every

time and he knows it. He used to be a
tough guy…now he is not so sure that
he is that tough. A loving wife has that
effect…he thought…to make him feel
on top of the world every time.
Even when he comes home feeling
tired and a bit cross with his
mates…he is usually smiling as soon as
his wife kissed him on the lips then the
cheeks…then she wipes the lipstick off.
The same thing every day. And that
perfume….it really turns him on every
time.
He forgets all his troubles after dinner
when he lay on the sofa, after a shower,
and put his head on her lap…as they
talk about everything. She strokes his
hair. Wayne usually excuses himself
after a short talk. They can hear him
strum his guitar from his room and
sing. His girlfriend still comes and goes.
She went back to Whangarei her Mum
is sick. She told them she will bring
some kina on Saturday for their usual
Sunday 'umu or hangi as Wayne calls it.
They usually have a 'umu on
Sundays…Manu and Wayne and the

boys always has one every Sunday. After they cover the 'umu, they all walk down the road to Church then take the food out after Church..usually 1-2 hours. It is perfectly cooked every time. The usual menu is taro, yams and various meats wrapped in taro leaves and coconut cream....called lu in Tongan or palusami in Samoan. The Samoan version does not have meat in it. Just the taro leaves and the coconut cream. There is also raw fish and kina or other seafood with fruits like watermelon, pineapple or mango.

Kiri loves their Sunday 'umu. She said it reminds her of when she was little…her grandfather used to make a hangi almost every week, to feed visitors or family members who visit from other cities and towns around New Zealand. Their farm was like a family marae for local and family gatherings.

"Why don't you invite your parents to come and visit one weekend and we will make us a umu?", Manu suggested.

"Yeah Kiri, that's a great idea", Wayne

added enthusiastically.

"Ok..I will call them"..she smiled at Manu and touches his cheek.

A week later…Mr and Mrs Rangi arrived on the Saturday afternoon. They decided to have breakfast and lunch at the farm then drove to Auckland to have dinner with Kiri and her husband and mate…then sleepover and lunch then drive back on the Sunday afternoon.

"Oh..it's so wonderful of you to come Mum and Dad", Kiri said as she kissed them on the cheeks after the usual hongi.

"Likewise Darling", her Mum said as she gave Manu a kiss on the cheek then wipe the lipstick off….then did the same with Wayne.

"Your flat looks really clean and tidy Kiri, you must be a good Mum already"…her Mum laughed and rubbed her tummy.

"Yeah…we used some of the wedding money to do up the flat and bought a car. We also did a lot of shopping for baby".

"How much money did you get from all the presents?", her Mum asked.

"More than $10,000 just under $11,000 plus lots of cutlery, bed sheets, blankets, glassware, pots, iron and a heap of other things as well. So we are well stocked. We put the rest of the money….about $6,000… in a joint account for a rainy day".

"Clever girl! That's a smart thing to do. You should start investing some money…maybe a property is a good idea", her father said smiling at her from the other sofa.

"Manu is also putting about $50 in the account every week. We hope to get a deposit for a house one day", Kiri smiled at her Dad.

"And how is the baby, dear?", her Mum asked.

"We don't know what the sex of the baby is yet…but the nurse said during my last visit to the hospital that I might be expecting in July", Kiri said radiant as usual.

"My God…that is only 3 months away!

Make sure you tell us as soon as the pain becomes regular. We want to drive over and meet the baby as soon as it is born, dear". Mrs Rangi continued.

"Sure, Mum".

"Why don't you guys talk while me and Manu prepare our barbecue on the back porch?", Wayne suggested.

"Yeah…sure, you guys go ahead", Mr Rangi smiled at Wayne.

"Honey, can you bring us some juice before you do the barbecue, please?", Kiri said to Manu.

"Yeah sure". Manu disappeared into the kitchen.

Wayne went into the backyard and started picking some of the taro leaves to make the lu for the Sunday umu. The boys had planted the taro from cuttings they got off some of the corms from the shops as well as their friend's gardens. During the winter the taro disappears as the frost destroys the leaves but the corms underground sprouts and grows quickly after winter. By the time it gets to Christmas the taro plants are already a metre high. The key is just plenty of water…and Wayne and Manu takes turns in watering their taro and vegetable garden once or twice a week. There was always plenty of firewood for the 'umu. They always come across free firewood piled on the side of the road and pick up some each week. People cut trees on their properties and just put them by the road, with a "free" sign, for anyone to take. They never use timber as they may be treated…chemicals that are used to treat timber might contaminate the food in the 'umu.

Manu also walked down the road to the fruitshop and bought some taro, kumara, coconuts, aluminium foil and onions for the 'umu. Everything was ready. Kiri did part of the shopping the day before. He started the fire for the 'umu, after taking all the stones out. Wayne got a few beers from the fridge and started the barbecue…sausages, patties and lamb chops…Mr and Mrs Rangi's favourite. Manu also put in some steaks for Wayne, himself and

Kiri who likes hers medium rare with lots of fresh vegies…. and some mussels as an appetizer. He got himself a coke.

"Fancy seeing you drinking coke mate", Wayne laughed.

"Yeah…I guess I am now a man with a collar", Manu chuckled….meaning his lay preacher status in church.

Wayne started strumming his guitar and humming to some unknown songs…it is his favourite spot with beer in one hand and guitar in the other.

Manu busied himself cooking the meat…he also put some foiled potatoes and kumara over the fire. They taste better that way…..according to Wayne. They setup a table and invited Mr and Mrs Rangi and Kiri outside. Wayne handed Mr Rangi a DB Brown.. "Call me Matiu"…he said to Manu and Wayne….it occurred to them, they have never been introduced by their first names until now. "And I am Mere", Kiri's Mum smiled.

"Cheers", Wayne lifted his beer and

toasted with everyone. Mere had a glass of red wine. Are you not drinking any alcohol Manu?", Mere asked…she has never heard of anyone not drinking alcohol in their circle of friends…even church people.

"Yeah…our Church frowns upon alcohol consumption. I used to drink alcohol but when I became a lay preacher.. I had to stop", Manu was feeling a bit uncomfortable explaining as he knows many Church goers in a lot of other Churches consume alcohol.

"That is very admirable Manu. We should come and attend the Church service when you preach next time", Mere continued.

"Yes, Mum…I will tell you when", Kiri suggested.

"Good, let's eat", Mere was already hungry or maybe it was the effect of the red wine.

"Don't worry dear. I'll get our plates", Matiu volunteered.

Manu and Wayne opened up the 'umu and the aroma was fantastic. Matiu and Mere came down to have a look. The steam coming out of the 'umu was still hot and they stepped back but enjoying the aroma of cooked meat mixed with the smell of steamed banana leaves covering it.

It was the first of many visits by Kiri's parents. They invited them to Whangarei for fishing trips and "eeling", which was laying an eel trap in a creek behind the farm. Manu was really surprised at the number of eels they got in that small creek! They smoked the eels and brought some to Kingsland. They sometimes got some fish too. Usually snapper and kahawai…when they put the trap in the mangroves near the sea. It gets 3 feet of water during high tide….and Matiu smoked the fish for their "work lunch" the following week. If they catch a lot of kahawai, they take up to 20 smoked fish to work and have a share lunch with the boys. It was always a "great occasion"…according to Wayne. When the big day arrived it did with a big bang! Manu and Wayne were driving to work. They were turning left into Bond Street from New North Road to go up to Great South Road when somebody crashed into them from behind. They both jumped out in a flash to check the damage. It was a pakeha kid!....probably in his teens…as drunk as a sheep on grass. The Ford was not damaged…it was build with some really strong and tough materials. The boy's car had a small dent at the front. Wayne pulled him out by the collar… "Sorry, sorry…my girlfriend kept pulling my hair…that's why". They looked into the Toyota…the girlfriend, who was also a pakeha, was also inebriated…she was just laughing her head off. Wayne told them off….swearing under his breath.

Manu told them to put their car by the road and they will drive them home they should not be driving around in that condition.

They pushed the Toyota to the side off the road and forced both kids into the back seat of their car. They refused to go back to their home so Manu and Wayne drove to the flat. Kiri was not there!

The neighbour came running in and told them the ambulance came and took Kiri to Auckland Hospital, she was having periodic pains.

"Alright you two. If you refuse to go home we'll take you with us to the hospital and hand you over to the Police!"…Wayne threatened.

"Whatever"…the girl said as she threw up in the car.

"Oh great! Just what we need at this time"…Wayne exclaimed in frustration.

John the neighbour, a pakeha man, volunteered to look after the 2 drunk teenagers while they go to the hospital.

"Thanks John…you are mate!"…Wayne gave John a pat on the back as they led the two drunks into their yard. The girl kept throwing up all over the house and on the footpath and even in John's yard.

"Call the Police and hand them over to them. They crashed into the back of our car. Their car is parked at the junction over there by the Methodist Church",

Wayne growled.

"Right oh, then", John agreed.

Wayne rang work and told them they are going to the hospital…Kiri is having the baby any minute. They will come in next morning. The news spread in a flash….everyone at work knew Manu's wife was expecting…the baby is arriving any day. They started a collection at work and somebody got a card for everyone to sign for Kiri and the baby. They even ordered a hundred roses from the farm down the road…to be delivered when Kiri and the baby comes home. The rose farmer was also at Southdown before he decided to grow roses…a huge flower market was growing in Auckland. They got a good discount.

Manu drove to the hospital. He was obviously nervous. The palms of his hands were really sweaty. He started humming.

Wayne could tell Manu was nervous…and he was humming "Po Malu" to calm himself. Wayne also hummed along…it has a miraculous calming effect on them. Luckily, the road wasn't crowded so they got to the hospital in half an hour. The receptionist told them to go straight to the Maternity Ward she was in room A7. They ran all the way up the stairs and found the room.

"What floor is this?", Manu asked Wayne.

"I am not sure…there, he pointed, it says Maternity on that sign… let's go in there".

The receptionist said only the husband can go in. "She is in labour".

"That's alright mate. You go in…I have a few phone calls to make", Wayne suggested.

Manu went in…just as the baby gave a huge howl as the Doctor gave him a pat on the back. He sucked in a lot of air then let out another mighty howl!

"My God….this is another Bavarotti", the Doctor chuckled as he passed the baby to the nurse… to wrap him in some a clean blanket.

The baby kept on howling…louder and louder…

Kiri was smiling tears running down her cheeks. She kept wiping her face and nose with the sheets, her makeup staining it. Then Manu realised he has been frozen by the door for a few seconds…maybe a minute…awed by what was transpiring before him…almost like a vision. He walked into the room.

"You must be the husband", the nurse smiled.

"Yes, I am".

She handed the baby to Manu…he smiled up at Manu through half closed eyes, as if he sensed him…no longer howling but sucking his thumb. Manu was in tears…

"He is smiling at me", he said to Kiri. "Come here, darling. Bring him over here".

Manu sat down on the edge of the bed and Kiri pulled his head down and kissed him on the lips then cheeks…then wiped the lipstick off. A kind of ritual that Manu is becoming used to. Manu gave her the baby.

"Oh…he's so handsome. Just like you

honey. He has your eyes and eyebrows. I think that nose and mouth is mine". She laughed....a high tinkling laugh...just like the fairies laugh. Manu thought. He is still awed by his wife's beauty.

The Doctor and nurses were clapping. They had just witnessed what makes all their hard toil and long hours worth it. The love shared by a couple who just had the greatest treasure you can ever hope for on this earth....a baby.

The Doctor and nurses gave Kiri a kiss on both cheeks...and the baby. They all wish them well and went out the door. "I'll come back later", one of the nurses said as she disappeared through the door closing it softly.

Wayne poked his head in...then tiptoed in and gave Kiri a kiss on the cheek. "Wow...he is huge!"...as he kissed the baby, then he laughed. Manu has never seen Wayne laugh like that before...a kind of laughter mixed with tears....as if he won the lotto or something. "Your parents and my girlfriend are on their way from

Whangarei…they should be here in about 10-20 minutes. They already left this morning. John called them'. Wayne said still looking with awe at the baby. "Good old John! Bless his soul", Kiri smiled at Manu. John, their neighbour, was an elderly man. He lived by himself. Kiri had given him her parent's number just in case something happened or she goes into labour and cannot call. She had called John to help her when she started having pains and John called the ambulance.

"Have you got a name for the baby?", Wayne asked as Kiri passed him the baby for a cuddle.

"Have you?", Kiri was looking at Manu.

"I….aah…yeah…it's William", Manu stuttered. He had thought about it already. It was his father's name. "William Latu junior".

"What a lovely name honey!", Kiri gave him another kiss. "William Latu, it is then".

"Hello, Mr William Latu Jr", Wayne was addressing the baby. "He is smiling at me!", Wayne gave another laugh. Manu realised how close he and Wayne had become…he is not only a friend but more like a brother. They have shared almost everything…and now he rejoices in his children.

Wayne had been a rough character, often mixing with the Black Power and Mongrel Mob in his youth. He smoked pot like cigarettes…every day. But since they started going to church Manu noticed he doesn't smoke anymore or even get drunk. He would have an occasional beer and sings more gospel music now…while strumming his guitar. He had cried when Tu'uta left….so there must have been a close bond between them, but he never mentioned it.

Mere poked her head in… "Hello!".
"Mum…come in", Kiri was almost shouting sitting up and adjusting her head pillows.. Her parents and Angela tiptoed in. Manu thought it must be some kind of Maori custom to tiptoe into a baby's room or something. Everyone seem to come in and tiptoe for some reason.

Mr and Mrs Rangi gave Kiri and Manu a hug and kiss then Wayne pass them William Latu Jr while he gave Angela a cuddle and a kiss.

Angela had a large bundle of red roses. She came over and gave them to Kiri and kissed her on the cheek.

"Congratulations darling. He is really lovely. Got your nose and mouth". Kiri let out a howl of laughter. "Exactly what I told Manu".

"Angela is right dear, William's got your nose and mouth", they all howled with laughter…while Manu was getting a bit lost. He did not quite understand.

"It's alright honey. They are just referring to my chatty nature and runny nose when I was little", Kiri patted Manu on the leg and smiled up at him.

Manu was crying. Tears were just running down his cheeks. He grabbed Kiri and hugged her…his huge shoulders heaving as he sobbed loudly.

"It's alright dear. Don't worry", Kiri patted him on the back as he continued to sob. Wayne went to the door and indicated with his head they should leave them alone for a few minutes. Kiri was getting concerned…Manu has been sobbing non-stop for 10 minutes already. She held him quietly, realising that maybe it's got something to do with his son in Tonga….George. He must be 6 years old now. There were 3 younger girls as well.

"Manu…are you crying because of your children in Tonga?", Kiri asked him pushing him away so she can look at his face. Manu just nodded and continued crying.

"What do you want me to do Manu?. I want to help them. Tell me darling, what can I do for them?", she was trying to look into his eyes but he was too busy wiping his face.

Manu tried to pull himself together. It seems to him this slender beautiful girl is a very strong woman. He could feel the determination in her voice. A kind of steel has crept into it.

"Do you want me to help them to move to New Zealand?", she asked. Manu nodded. He had stopped crying but was still looking at the floor. "Alright, my darling…I will help your children…our children", she said quietly as she pulled his head to her chest and kept stroking his hair. "I will help our children, Manu", she whispered…with emotion in her voice.

Chapter Seven....

THE REUNION

It has been 5 months since Kiri and baby William were back at the Kingsland flat. He was getting really chubby and starting to form words…making baby sounds…still a bit gibberish…but it showed he is a very alert and healthy baby. Kiri always buy fresh fish, pumpkin and vegetables and cook and mash them for William. He was still breast fed as well. She wants her baby to have the best…and he was.

The $6,000 dollars, collected from presents at the wedding, had grown to $7,000 and Kiri was seriously considering buying the flat. She had talked to the landlord and he was keen to sell. It was actually the old man next door, John. He was the landlord! He told her to talk to the bank…but he is willing to give them a "rent to own" arrangement. He has decided to go travelling around the world. Since his wife Olivia died 2 years before he was saving a bit of money "to go and forget his loss in the wonders of the world", he says.

Kiri has been busy ringing the Immigration Department….enquiring about the best way to bring Manu's children to New Zealand. Manu has written to Heilala and asked her to forgive him…but the best way for the kids is to move to New Zealand and live with him.

Heilala cried again for a whole day. God has taken her husband…now he is going to rip her heart out as well. Their children was her only condolence after Manu left her. She blames God for her misfortune. She goes to Church every Sunday and prays loudly…and cries…and confess everything in front of the whole church…what they call "talaloto"..in the Free Wesleyan Church … "pouring your heart out"...now the whole town knows what is going on. She looked old and wretched for her 33 years. The past year has been a lifetime of torture in her eyes....her husband was her life...her children were her breath....now ripped away from her...by God. She was beyond comforting.

The Minister and the Church collected $2,000 and gave them to Heilala to help her family. They brought food, fish and meat every day to her house and prayed...and cried...but she grew thinner each day. Then one morning she failed to wake up.

Manu wailed so loudly that John came running from next door. He thought something had happened to William. "No...it was his ex-wife in Tonga...she died", Kiri said. "His 6 year old son George told him on the phone. Heilala just grew thinner every day and one morning they woke up to find her dead. When the neighbours came the youngest girl…who was 3 years old was still trying to wake her up. That's why he cried".

"Just let me know if I can help", the old man offered touching baby Williams head. He was very fond of the baby.

"Thanks John", was all Kiri can say. She knows his loneliness since Olivia died and her heart aches for him. She watched the old man walking back to his house, from her doorway. There seem to be a noticeable limp when he walks.

"I like that old man", Manu said quietly from behind her.

"Yeah, he needs some companionship, I think".

"I will invite him for a drink sometime".

"Sure darling, we should", Kiri smiled and kissed him. Manu is such a nice man, she thought.

"Manu, I think we should go to your ex-wife's funeral. I have the forms. We can adopt your children and bring them with us to New Zealand. We can take some of the money….don't worry I am not ashamed to go to the funeral and pay my respects. I will be proud to call your family and hers my own", Kiri put her arms around Manu while holding William with the other. Manu just nodded. His eyes has become red from crying….but he can feel the comfort of her arm around him. This small woman…so frail looking…and beautiful…with the strength of a thousand men.

John came back with 2 cups of coffee and some biscuits and put them on the coffee table.

"I thought I'd make myself useful. Since Olivia died I haven't made any tea or coffee. So I thought they will come in handy".

"Thanks John. You are a saint. When you die I will propose to the Pope to make you a saint", Kiri smiled.

John laughed so loudly that Manu could not help smiling as well. The old man is very fond of her. She has a way with men. Her kind hearted ways has won everyone over.

A week later they were on an Air New Zealand Boeing 737 to Tonga. The nurse said William was old enough to fly with them so it was just a matter of packing their stuff and buying the plane ticket. Kiri withdrew $4,000 to take with them. They had worked out the airfare for the 4 kids plus their stay in Tonga…hopefully everything will be alright.

They celebrated the night before…Manu got a letter from the Department of Immigration confirming his permanent resident status has been granted by the Minister. So there is some good coming out of this…as well…Manu thought. Kiri has been a blessing beyond imagination. She kept him smiling when his world was crumbling.

They arrived in Tonga on a hot Saturday afternoon…in December. Almost everyone were wearing black and ta'ovala or wrap around mat. Some so big that it covers their heads as well. Manu explained they are the people doing the work…boiling the water and making the umu. Heilala's brother's family. The large ta'ovala signifies their low status …hence their assigned work in the "kitchen", cooking and so on. In Tongan culture the sister has higher rank than the brother.

Kiri was like a star visiting Tonga. The whole suburb of Pahu turned up to see her. She has stolen their "man" and they want to see what she is like. The word of Manu's divorce and wedding to her had intrigued everyone.

Kiri looked really stunning in black
with her ta'ovala…and holding baby
William as she emerged from the
arrival lounge. Manu was respected in
the village…a kind of ironman…who
seemed to excel at everything. So it was
a surprise to everyone that he would
leave his family for another woman. He
was walking beside her pushing their
bags on a trolley…smiling and kissing
his relatives as they rush over and
embrace him…some were crying
loudly..as both families let their grief
out. Not so much the death of Heilala
but over the loss of his mana…as
Wayne puts it. But after looking at the
girl and the baby, they changed their
minds. She is now the new Princess of
the family. They all want to kiss and
embrace this brave girl who comes to
his ex-wife's funeral.

Every store and house by the road
were playing Christmas carols in
Tongan and English as they drove to
Nuku'alofa…the window of the Ford
Fairmont was down and William Sr

was driving at like…20 km per hour while he talks. Even the bicycles were faster…as Kiri joked later. It was a huge car and so spacious inside and it drives like the aeroplane! So quiet and smooth.

Kiri was so surprised at how friendly the people were. She had expected to be shown the cold shoulder by Heilala's family. But they heard of what happened and how she wants to adopt the kids and take them with her to New Zealand…so they really warmed to her. There is no use crying over spilt milk….the Minister had said in last Sunday's sermon in Church.

Manu's family embraced her with open arms. William Sr and Mary had prepared the spare room for them. It was fairly spacious. Just two single beds and nothing else in the room. They joined them together to make a double bed.

Manu's kids took turns in carrying the

baby and kissing him. "Careful you lot...don't touch the baby you might "dirty him" ...they all laughed...especially the kids...Mary has taken over as William's protector. Manu noticed the kids have grown a bit taller since he last saw them. They would come and sit on his lap for hours...looking up at him regularly to check if he is still there.

After the funeral, they went to the New Zealand High Commission Office in Nuku'alofa to finalise the kid's adoption papers. They were told everything are in order...their permanent residence were stamped on their passports. Manu bought their plane tickets...everything was ready.

They had a feast that Sunday at the Pahu Wesleyan Church and Manu, Kiri, the kids and baby William were invited. William Sr and Mary drove them from Longolongo to Pahu for the feast.

"Careful Kiri don't eat too much or you

might get fat", Mary advised to hysterical laughter from the kids. A kind of standing joke in the family. Kiri laughed. She was really warming to Mary's kind of humour.

They sat at the front. It was the usual feasts they have in New Zealand as well. Kiri was used to the Church Feasts at Kingsland. Rows of suckling pigs, heaps of food and drink and plenty of singing and praying….and speeches. All good…she always enjoy them…especially those hymns…they just sound divine!

Heilala's family gave Kiri a present of ngatu. It was a "launima"…the largest single piece of tapa used in traditional gift giving. It weighs…probably 50-70 kgs…about 30 metres long and 10 metres wide… beautifully decorated with traditional art. They said…Heilala made it for her children…now it yours. Kiri was so moved by their gesture it was her turn to cry…it was like they are giving her a part of Manu's ex-wife to take to New Zealand.

It was evening when they said the closing prayers….they did not turn the light on but had candles lit all around the Church. Manu's four kids will perform an item for the last time in their Church before they fly to New Zealand. They are going to do a drama of the birth of Christ…the very first Christmas….while the whole Church…some 2-300 hundred of them sang Po Malu… Silent Night. Kiri could not hold her tears…she has also become as emotional as them. This song has meant so much to her…it is like the song of her heart. Her very first Christmas when she…like in a trance…stoned from marijuana and beer heard the song and saw this man…her husband. Something told her to kiss him and she did…and her whole world changed.

Her love for him has changed her life. She now has feelings that she thought she never needed. It is something really wonderful and magical...crowned by the birth of their son...baby William. She just feel so blessed...in the darkness of that Church 2,000 miles away from her home....among strangers...who touched her...really, really deep inside.

The next week was filled in with sightseeing and meeting more and more of Manu's family. There were feasts almost every day until they were ready to leave. Kiri had asked Manu to send their ngatu and other gifts by air cargo. They could not carry them on the plane.

When the big day arrived, they had to hire a bus to take them to the airport. There were so many people who want to see them off at the airport. There was much kissing, well wishing and more crying before they finally flew out of Fua'amotu airport, all seven of them. Manu's kids...now their kids...were so excited to fly on a plane to New Zealand.

William Sr and Mary were crying as they waved to the plane. William held a photo album…a gift from Kiri. The very first photo filled the whole page… of Manu, Kiri and baby William smiling, in their living room surrounded by a 100 red roses.

Wayne met them at the airport…he had hired a van so they can all fit in. They had driven back in silence then…

"John had left…on what he calls his big OE", Wayne said. He left an A4 envelope for you". He handed it to Kiri. It had "For Manu, Kiri, William and the kids"…written on it. "I don't think he will come back. I found the envelope as I came back from work. He just pushed it in under the door".

It was the Deed for both houses. John had wrote… "Dear Manu and Kiri, Olivia and I had always wanted to do something grand while we were still alive. We did not get around to it. You have blessed me with your lives and so I am sure Olivia will agree with me. I finally get to do something grand…this is the "Deed of Ownership" for both houses. They are yours now. Just sign the dotted line in front of a JP and get your lawyer to do the rest… I am sure the properties will give your loving family a good start in life. I may not be back but keep me in your prayers.

John.

"Oh John…Kiri cried again…you didn't have to do that"…as she rocked William on her lap.

They got home and ordered some KFC. Kiri thought it will cheer Manu's kids up. And it did… "those 11 herbs by the Colonel always do wonders for hungry kids"…she says.

Tears came easily to Kiri and Manu for a few more days before they settled down. They realise how much John had given them…and they wonder about the old man travelling alone… "to forget his loss"..he said.

Wayne and the family planned a party for William and the kids to meet everyone that weekend. Kiri read John's letter for everyone to hear. Apparently the properties are worth about $300,000, she added. They all clapped and sang …"for he's a jolly good fellow" many times.

Manu's kids have forgotten the past already…they seem to enjoy that moment much more than any other moment in their short lives. The youngest kid kept looking up at his face, as she sat on his lap, just to make sure he is still there. Kiri noticed it too and wiped another tear from her face.

THE END…

EPILOGUE

"So that is what happened", George looked around the kava circle. They were all wiping their eyes. It seems to be a Tongan custom... "crying for just about any reason".. he joked. They just smiled.... "let's have another drink"...his cousin Tesi joked to liven up the atmosphere.

The Kolokakala Club was a fairly large Kava Club and members usually top 50 every night. George had spent the whole day and part of the evening telling them their family's story. Some of his relatives come from the village of Mu'a which is further divided into Tatakamotonga and Lapaha villages, as the population grows.

His PhD work has been completed. George will be leaving for New Zealand the following week to write it up and take a break. His younger sisters

'Amelia, Latai and Sela are also at the University of Auckland. William will join them next year. There are two younger brothers...Wilson and Dee are still at High School.

Manu and Kiri are spending most of their time travelling to the islands of the Pacific...the kids run their little dairy in Kingsland by New North Road. They decided to build one when Southdown closed down and it would be good business training for the children, Kiri reasoned.

It is a bit larger than most dairies. Their properties...a present from John their neighbour are now worth in excess of $1 million. They live in one and rent out the other. They did get another postcard from John he is running a little motel in a seaside village in Scotland...apparently he met "somebody that looks like Olivia over there".

Kiri also inherited her parent's 400 hectare farm which is worth in excess of $10 million. Wayne and Angela are leasing it from her. Wayne also married Angela and they have 6 kids.

All the relatives are so proud of the kids. They know who the primary force in their lives is....a slender, brown eyed, beautiful and smart woman with long black hair...Kiri TePou Latu.

GLOSSARY OF NON-ENGLISH WORDS.

1.   Hangi – an earth oven in the Maori language...also called 'umu in the Samoan and Tongan languages.

2.   Puha – a wild Maori vegetable...it is sometimes used loosely to refer to three species collected from cultivated areas...*Solanum sp.*, *Amaranthus sp*, and another resembling *Sonchus sp* and dandelions.

3.   Kumara – sweet potato in Maori

4.   Po Malu – the Tongan name for the Christmas carol Silent Night.

5.   Mokopuna – grandchildren in the Maori and Tongan languages.

6.   Kaumatu'a – Maori elders

7.   Heilala – a fragrant flowering plant in Tonga. It is also used as a name for women.

8.   "E 'eiki keke to'o ho mau loungutu"..a part of the morning Church Service in the

Tongan Free Wesleyan Church or Methodist. It literally means..."Lord remove our sinners lips".

9. Mana – a word in the Maori language that refers to the "aura" or dignity and respect that leaders have.

10. Pakeha – Maori word for European.

11. Palusami – a Samoan delicacy made of coconut cream wrapped in taro (*Colocasia* sp.) leaves.

12. Lu – a Tongan dish made of meat, onions, coconut cream wrapped in taro (*Colocasia* sp or *Xanthosoma* sp.) leaves.

13. Marae – Maori meeting ground including a meeting house and greens (lawn).

14. Kahawai – a common fish in New Zealand resembling mackerel.

15.Talaloto – a public confession in the Tongan Free Wesleyan Church during afternoon prayers accompanied by hymns.

16. Ta'ovala – large wrap around mat to show respect during traditional meetings

or gatherings including funerals in
Tongan communities.

Author's background...

 Semisi Pule also known as Semisi Pule Pone was born in the Kingdom of Tonga in 1961. He attended Primary School at G.P.S Longolongo from 1967 to 1973. He passed the inter-college examination and entered his chosen Tonga High School from 1974 to 1979. He passed his Tonga Higher leaving Certificate in 1977, New Zealand School Certificate in 1978 (5 subjects) and New Zealand University Entrance in 1979 (5 subjects). After completing Form 7 at Mt Albert Grammar School in 1980 he entered the University of Auckland in 1981, graduating with a Bachelor of Science in 1984, with ceremony in May, 1985. He returned to

Tonga in June, 1985 and joined the
Ministry of Agriculture, Fisheries and
Forests (MAFF) as an Agriculture
Officer specializing in Plant Pathology.
He also completed a Master of Science
(Hons) from the University of Auckland
in 1988, graduating in 1989, and was
promoted to Senior Plant Virologist,
with MAFF Tonga, in 1991.

He joined the University of the South
Pacific, Agriculture Campus in Apia,
Samoa in March, 1992 as a Fellow in
Tissue Culture with the European
Union funded Project 7, Tissue Culture,
under the auspices of the Institute for
Research, Extension and Training in
Agriculture (IRETA).

His job was to help disseminate and
store popular germplasm of Pacific
crops, *in vitro*. He also did a lot of
research published in his book **Plant
Protection in the Pacific 3, tissue
culture**.

In June 1993, he joined the South

Pacific Commission (SPC) as the Plant Protection Advisor and Head/Co-ordinator of the Plant Protection Service. During his time with SPC he was appointed as an expert on Biosecurity (phytosanitary measures) with the Food and Agriculture Organisation of the United Nations (7 years) and also a member of the Technical Consultation among Regional Plant Protection Organizations which meets in Rome every two years.

His work in the Pacific Islands in the field of Plant Protection are published in his series of books called **Plant Protection in the Pacific, books 1-4.** There are 3 more books, in Plant Protection, being planned.

He migrated to New Zealand in June 1996 where he was involved with various businesses. He is now a writer of children's stories, novels, poetry and humour and has published more than 200 books and ebooks in amazon.com and blurb.com.

Author's comments...

This book is aimed at adult reading and
entertainment but also an aid for
Pacific Island students who study
English literature. The objective is to
say something about the reasons why
people migrate from the Pacific Islands,
in this case Tonga, and also the
associated problems of leaving their
families behind.

It is usually the men who leave the wife
and kids in the islands, but on certain
occasions women too are known to
leave their families in the islands.

Although the men suffer from guilt and
isolation emotions...for example...."
'Aisea and Manu crying in the backyard
under the influence of alcohol"...most
find refuge in the Churches....in this
case the Methodist Church. Overstaying
their visa was another problem caused
by some men's desire to get permanent

residence through amnesty.

In reality, it is true that the Pacific Church leaders play an important role in helping Pacific Islanders settle in New Zealand and giving them a social structure and community which helps tremendously. The continuation of culture through church activities like "feasting", "fund raising " and other avenues help immensely...with their feeling of belonging to their new community.

In the case of the main character in this fictitious story, Manu leaving Heilala for Kiri...it does happen to many married Pacific Island men and women. Some leave for love others for "material" reasons. Kiri's acceptance by Manu and Heilala's family at her funeral and the emotion of it all is also very typical of Tongan families and how they cope with loss of a family member. Children are usually the casualties in the broken relationships.

John's act of kindness is also typical of many wealthy "pakeha" who want to help Pacific Island people they have come to know as friends. For example, pakeha individuals bringing the islanders to work in New Zealand to raise money. Employing a large number of islanders is another.

The story aim to highlight the lives of the characters and spend little time on discussing their environment, friends, family, dwelling, roads and so on....It is left to the readers imagination to "fill in the details"...also the "missing years" after the kids arrive in New Zealand.

Some of the techniques in writing this story will become apparent as you read it...like the use of "recollections". For example, Manu's visa...his third extension wasn't mentioned until late in the story. Tu'uta and 'Aisea's departure are two other examples. Nothing is mentioned of them until later in the story. The 100 roses bought by Manu's mates for Kiri was never mentioned again until the end of the story...where it appeared in the album, a present from Manu and Kiri for William and Mary. The idea is to connect the story similar to tying a rope around bits and pieces on a truck so they don't fall off during the journey. I feel it worked well, similar to telling a story to your children and relatives and answering questions about "gaps" in it. It helps to 'put the story together' in the readers mind, I think.

The reader who is not familiar with Pacific Island culture will no doubt find the story "interesting". Since trading began between the Pacific Islands and New Zealand, Australia and the United States in the early 20th century...a steady stream of migrants have moved to those metropolitan centres tolive permanently and they help to bring friends and relatives over. Those migrants returned to the islands, for holidays, with stories of "riches" and better opportunities which fueled desires by the youth to migrate overseas. Very often they leave on a visitor's visa and get married or "overstay" to try and get permanent residence when governments offer amnesty. They, in turn, bring their families and old people which add to the rapid expansion of the islander population in those 3 countries. Tongans overseas, for example, now outnumber Tongans in Tonga. There are 100,000 Tongans in Tonga.

It has become a financial bonanza for the country as a whole. Overseas Tongans send about $TOP 200-300 million in cash and goods, to relatives in Tonga every year; and it is growing.

Although there are many "events" in the story....the main plot should be Manu's wedding and divorce. The story revolve around his romance and marriage with Kiri and his divorce from Heilala and the resulting fallout. The point is his desire to get permanent residence and bring his family to New

Zealand. Unfortunately, Heilala was an acceptable "casualty", probably because he fell in love with Kiri; which was not part of his plan. The use of the carol "Po Malu" or "Silent Night" to set the tone and emotion of the story is deliberate...it is a favourite of mine. Millions of people around the world sing or play it at Christmas and probably appropriate for Manu and Kiri to meet during the song.

Despite the climax being the funeral of Heilala and 'bringing the kids to New Zealand', the expected "meeting of Kiri and Heilala's family"...it was more emotional than a confrontation. In many situations like this, in the islands, often there is obvious friction between the new wife and the ex-wife's family.

I propose the theme as "love conquers all". Despite the problems, Manu and Kiri's love for each other endured and his kids were brought to New Zealand where the whole family prospered.

I hope these comments will be useful for the readers whether they are students of literature or not. There are still many other "gems" to discover in the story, which I shall leave for the readers to find.

www.ingramcontent.com/pod-product-compliance
Lightning Source LLC
Chambersburg PA
CBHW021222260626
47172CB00002B/557